© 1993 Geddes & Grosset

First published 1993 by Geddes & Grosset,
David Dale House, New Lanark ML11 9DJ, Scotland
Reprinted 1994, 1996, 2001

ISBN 1 85534 581 1

Printed and bound in China

The Gingerbread Man

Retold by Judy Hamilton
Illustrated by Lindsay Duff

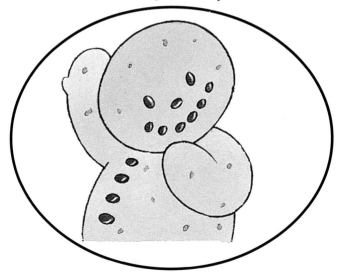

Tarantula Books

There was once an old woman who loved baking. Whenever she had time, she would set to work. Bread or cakes, pies or buns; she always enjoyed baking, and her husband, the taster, had a jolly good time as well. One day, the old woman was baking gingerbread. The kitchen was filled with the delicious smell of treacle and spices. The old woman made enough mixture to make three big loaves of gingerbread and when she had filled the baking tins, she had a little left over, so she moulded the sticky mixture into the shape of a little man. Then she added currant eyes, nose, and mouth, and gave him four little currant buttons down his front. "This will be a nice surprise for my husband," she thought.

When the old man came home from work, he sniffed the warm air in the kitchen. The old woman winked at him and said:

"I've made some gingerbread, and there's an extra surprise in the oven. It should be ready now!" She opened the oven and took out the loaves of gingerbread. Then she lifted out the gingerbread man.

"A gingerbread man!" smiled her husband. "What a lovely surprise! I shall eat him after my supper."

At these words, the gingerbread man came to life. He jumped to his feet and declared loudly:

"Oh no, you WON'T!" Then he jumped down from the table and ran out of the kitchen door.

The old couple gave chase at once. But the gingerbread man was too fast for them.

"Run, run, as fast as you can!" he cried. "You can't catch me, I'm the gingerbread man!"

On and on he ran, as fast as his gingerbread legs could carry him. A dog lying on a doorstep by the roadside saw the gingerbread man as he went past.

"A gingerbread man! Very tasty!" he thought, and joined in the chase. But the gingerbread man only laughed at him: "Run, run as fast as you can! You can't catch me, I'm the gingerbread man! I can run faster than the old woman and the old man, and I can run faster than you, I can!"

The dog ran after him, but he could not catch the gingerbread man.

On through the streets ran the gingerbread man, with the old woman, the old man and the dog still chasing after him. As he ran, he passed by a boy kicking stones along the road. When he saw the gingerbread man, the boy stopped.

"A gingerbread man!" he exclaimed. "I would love to eat that!"

So the boy began to chase the gingerbread man as well. But the gingerbread man was not worried. He only laughed:

"Run, run, as fast as you can! You can't catch me I'm the gingerbread man! I can run faster than the dog, the old woman and the old man, and I can run faster than you, I can!" The boy ran fast, but couldn't catch the gingerbread man.

The gingerbread man ran on, chased by the old woman, the old man, the dog and the boy. Soon he passed by two road-menders, busily digging a hole. When they saw the gingerbread man, they dropped their shovels and ran after him.

"A gingerbread man! Just what we need for our tea!" they cried.

But the gingerbread man only laughed:

"Run, run, as fast as you can! You can't catch me, I'm the gingerbread man! I can run faster than the boy, the dog, the old woman and the old man, and I can run faster than you, I can!" The road-menders were fit and strong, but they still could not catch the gingerbread man.

The chase continued, with the old woman, the old man, the dog, the boy and the road-menders all running after the gingerbread man. They ran right through the town and out into the countryside. Soon they passed a horse, grazing in a field. The horse saw the gingerbread man and licked his lips.

"A gingerbread man! That would make a nice change from grass!" said the horse, jumping over the fence and galloping after the gingerbread man.

But, as always, the gingerbread man only laughed. "Run, run, as fast as you can! You can't catch me, I'm the gingerbread man! I can run faster than the road-menders, the boy, the dog, the old woman and the old man, and I can run faster than you, I can!"

And on he ran.

The gingerbread man was right. The horse was young but not even his fastest gallop was as fast as the gingerbread man. Along the country roads they ran; the old woman, the old man, the dog, the boy, the road-menders and the horse all chasing the gingerbread man. The gingerbread man laughed as he ran like the wind. He knew he was safe, for none of them was fast enough to catch him.

"Run, run!" he called out gleefully. "Run, run, as fast as you can! You can't catch me, I'm the gingerbread man!"

And those that ran after him puffed and panted more and more, as they tried in vain to catch him

The gingerbread man turned off the road and began to run through the fields, skipping and jumping over tussocks of grass. He never seemed to be tiring. He never seemed to be running short of breath. When he came to a fence, he leapt over it and carried on running. When he came to a tree or a bush, he dodged round it and carried on. And still he laughed. The old woman, the old man, the dog, the boy, the road-menders and the horse chased after him still, but they were getting further behind, and could not carry on much longer.

Then, all of a sudden, the gingerbread man stopped in his tracks. He had come to the banks of a river. The river was deep and fast-flowing, and too wide to jump across.

The gingerbread man did not know what to do. There was no bridge in sight to help him to get across. And he could not swim, for the water would soak into his gingerbread body and turn him to mush. The old woman, the old man, the dog, the boy, the road-menders and the horse were still coming after him, so he could not go back.

"What shall I do?" he said. "I have to run as fast as I can! They must not catch the gingerbread man!"

At that moment, the gingerbread man heard a silky-smooth voice in his ear:

"I can help you to get across the river, if you like!" The gingerbread man turned round and saw a fox standing beside him, with a smile to match his silky-smooth voice.

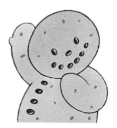

"Jump onto my back and I'll carry you across the river," said the fox.

The gingerbread man did not think twice. He jumped onto the fox's back. The fox stepped into the river. "Don't get me wet!" said the gingerbread man.

Then he turned to the old woman, the old man, the dog, the boy, the road-menders and the horse, who were approaching the riverbank.

"Run, run, as fast as you can! You can't catch me, I'm the gingerbread man!"

The fox waded out towards the middle of the river.

"The water's getting deeper now," he told the gingerbread man. "You had better climb a little higher up my back."

Obediently, the gingerbread man did so.

The fox took a few steps more into the river.

"The water is getting deeper still," he warned the gingerbread man. "You had better climb up onto my neck!"

Once again, the gingerbread man did as the fox told him without asking any questions. The fox waded further into the water.

"Watch out!" he told the gingerbread man. "It's getting really deep now! Climb up onto my head!"

The gingerbread man did as he was told and turned back to look at the riverbank.

"You can't catch me, I'm the gingerbread man!" he called out to the old woman, the old man, the dog, the boy, the road-menders and the horse, who were now standing on the riverbank, watching.

They watched as the fox waded right into the middle of the river. And they listened as the fox spoke to the gingerbread man one more time:

"It's still too deep! Climb onto the tip of my nose!"

The old woman, the old man, the dog, the boy, the road-menders and the horse all watched as the gingerbread man climbed up onto the tip of the fox's nose. And they watched as the fox tossed the gingerbread man up in the air and caught him with a snap of his jaws. The gingerbread man was gone in one gulp.

"Well," said the old woman."That's the last time I make one of those!"

The fox smiled. He knew that you had to be smart to catch a gingerbread man!